A ROOKIE READER

PANCAKES, CRACKERS, AND PIZZA

A BOOK ABOUT SHAPES

By Marjorie Eberts and
Margaret Gisler

Illustrations by Stephen Hayes

Prepared under the direction of Robert Hillerich, Ph.D.

CHILDRENS PRESS ™
CHICAGO

To our mothers

Library of Congress Cataloging in Publication Data

Eberts, Marjorie.
Pancakes, crackers, and pizza.

(A Rookie reader)
Summary: The things that Eddie loves to eat all come in different shapes. Includes a word list.
[1. Shape—Fiction. 2. Food—Fiction. 3. Vocabulary]
I. Gisler, Margaret. II. Hayes, Steven, ill.
III. Hillerich, Robert L., 1927- IV. Title.
V. Series.
PZ7.E194Pan 1984 [E] 84-7699
ISBN 0-516-02063-3

10 11 12 13 14 15 16 17 18 19 R 02 01 00 99 98 97 96 95 94

This is Eddy.

Eddy likes to eat, and eat, and eat.

CEREAL
DOUGHNUTS

Eddy eats round things.

Eddy eats pancakes,

oranges,

and eggs.

Eddy eats square things.

Eddy eats crackers,

CRACKERS
CRACKERS
C

meat,

and cheese.

Eddy eats triangles.

Eddy eats pizza,

salad,

and watermelon.

Eddy eats circles,

and squares,

and triangles.

Eddy eats all shapes.

Eddy eats, and eats, and eats.

Eddy looks

like what he eats.

WORD LIST

all
and
cheese
circles
crackers
eat
eats
Eddy
eggs
he
is
like
likes
looks
meat
oranges
pancakes
pizza
round
salad
shapes
square(s)
things
this
to
triangles
watermelon
what

About the Authors

Marjorie Eberts and **Margaret Gisler** have spent the last few years collaborating on books dealing with the language arts. Both have had experience as teachers and have masters degrees in reading from Butler University. This is their first Rookie Reader.

About the Artist

Stephen Hayes is a free-lance, humorous illustrator from Cincinnati, Ohio. He received his degree in Fine Arts from Miami University in Oxford, Ohio. Steve has illustrated humorous greeting cards and several books for children. This book is dedicated to his wife, Susan, and his daughter, Sarah.